THE 7TH MAN

:　　　:

MELANIE RAE THON

THE 7TH MAN

:   :

MELANIE RAE THON

NEW MICHIGAN PRESS

TUCSON, ARIZONA

NEW MICHIGAN PRESS

DEPT OF ENGLISH, P. O. BOX 210067

UNIVERSITY OF ARIZONA

TUCSON, AZ 85721-0067

<http://newmichiganpress.com>

Orders and queries to nmp@thediagram.com.

ISBN 978-1-934832-52-3. FIRST PRINTING.

Printed in the United States of America.

Design by Ander Monson.

Cover image © Defun | Dreamstime.com—
Micrograph Of Blood Vessel, Artery Photo

CONTENTS

:   :

You can't believe how graceful we are, six men moving as
one, each sensing all others—but not watching: the eye
need not see the hand to know how the hand moves, to
feel what the hand is doing:

We are watching the 7th man, the one between, the
heart at the center, the one who brings us here, strange
and beautiful: we are dancing the man down the hall,
strapping the man to the gurney:

He's not the real man—not Leonard Loy Hayes, not
Aureo Montoya—not today, not this hour—not one of
the many gone and still to come: no, one of us today:

Mick Delaney, a small man with terrible strength:
vein in the neck popping blue, dark vein in the temple
throbbing:

That bounce off the ball of the foot—he likes to be the
one, moving six men to his rhythm:

Mitchell Dean Delaney, a man we know but pretend not
to know—the accused, the condemned—he killed his
wife and her mother, dumped three bodies in a ditch,
doused a living man with gasoline, set a man not dead
on fire—desecrator of human life, human waste to be
excreted:

I've walked 131 men down this hall—strapped the chests
of 29—left leg, right shoulder—secured the pelvises of
40 men:

You learn things about a man, feel the blood running
through him:

Helped to unstrap and lift 131 human bodies: fathers,
sons, brothers, uncles—loved or unloved, claimed,
disposable—gone from this earth: cause of death, legal
homicide:

There will be no body today, only Mick with his eyes
closed, Mick strapped tight and still twitching, a man
we love—yes, *love*—but men among men never say this:

Mick says, *I do have some last words—I'll tell you
later*—a joke, *yes*, as if, *later*: Mick, our friend, whose
children played with our children, whose wife whispered
with our wives—in the garden, in the kitchen—she
knows secrets about us:

Our fears, our failures—love here is not a useful
emotion—not in the performance, not in the rehearsal,
the 7th of 77 times we will follow the steps, observe the
protocol:

Till we can do it in our sleep, till we are doing it in our
sleep, again and all night, dreaming ourselves into death:

Over and over:

Till the curtains part and we are gone—unknown,
unnamed—actors erased from the stage:

We will not be accused, not held accountable:

Riley goes limp and we have to drag him—95 seconds
down the hall, 67 more to hoist him on the gurney—
we need to be prepared: Riley Ferrell, 187 pounds of
resistance—a mass to be moved—he's swearing like
a man about to die, like a man afraid we'll kill him—
words I've never heard him say—wild conflagrations—
all those images burning in my brain:

Do not turn away, do not be distracted:

I have the left leg, Troy straps the pelvis—Mick presses
hard on the ribs—Everett pulls the chest strap:

Fear now will not stop, remorse here will not save you:

We are breath inside a breath, the 7th man's last gasp,
sweat on skin, heat, our hands here and here, the smell
of smoke, buckles tightening:

The 7th man knows what we've done—*your hands*, who
we are, *on me*—but will not waste his breath to blame:

No, he says crazy things, *I forgive*, or, *you've been kind*—
he says, *thank you:*

The one laid out, the one on the gurney, the soon to be
dead man is already singing, *as long as life endures:*

Strange, that voice, *amazing grace*, lower than his
speaking voice, moving into me:

We know this man—we watched him all afternoon—
we brought him his dinner—nothing special, not since
one man ordered and refused to eat: chicken-fried steak,
mashed potatoes: *with every breath*—he dumped and
flushed—*I defy you:*

Now they take what we serve—faded peas, bleached
bread—something brown resembling meatloaf: we
watched him eat: hand to mouth, every mouthful:

We hosed him down, we saw him naked:

He's been singing all day—we made him bend, we
watched him open:

We looked inside—he looked just like us:

How sweet the sound, into my ear, touching my
eardrum—all day, *my fears relieved:*

He made the most amazing sounds—with his body,
with his breath: wind moving through, lips vibrating:

His whole body trembling into song—a trombone:

He tried to teach me—I sputtered and spit: the sound
was impossible:

Left wrist, right ankle, *the sun forbear to shine, but God,*
the places we touched—here and here—those hands,
those fingers, *forever mine,* my hand on his back as we
walked, cell to gurney:

I am forbidden to touch—unless to take down, to
subdue or lift, unless to drag, unless necessary:

A man has a choice: a man has his freedom:

Convinced, coerced: he wants to walk like a man: he
intends to cooperate, *my hope secures,* die like a man,
keep his dignity:

The warden is the 8th man, the eyes of all, watching
our spines, *the Lord has promised good to me*, hesitation
of the hip, my hands, *I once was lost*, murmur of the
heart—*Officer Arnoux*—the warden wakes me:

But the hand that touched can't untouch, *and now am
found*, the voice that entered shall not cease:

The 7th man feels it now, the heat of the hand, my palm
pressed to his back, firm and tender, not to push, but to
reassure, to keep him strong, to keep us moving:

Twelve years he's known what only God should know,
exactly when:

Now the day has come at last, the hour of dusk, the
moment:

The clock on the wall glows green, 6:07:

Minutes now are everything, *the earth shall soon dissolve*,
a man doesn't want to go limp, *wives whispering*, doesn't
want to lose his legs, wants to sing, pretend he's one of
us, pretend we're only practicing:

We are practicing—numbers fizz and hum, time
vibrates:

:   :

We take turns as the 7th man because no body is the
same and every man responds differently:

Neville Trace, blessing us in his mind—to keep
himself calm, to keep the legs steady—a mountain
of a man, Neville: he could bring us down with one
breath, the chest suddenly huge, arms stretched wide,
wings whirling—he could destroy: the mass of a man
converting to energy:

He fills the space between, he fills the gurney:

6:09, we see the pulse of his enormous heart, *here*,
beneath the shirt: the heart, the ribs, the blood
throbbing:

Rivers of blood, the surge of Neville's blood, the blood
of a man this size could drown us:

Beautiful the way we move, the way the mind travels,
out of itself, into another: the way I know where every
man is, what each hand is doing:

Strange the way I love these men, as the hand loves the
heart, without thinking—the body not mine alone, but
part of many:

My hand on the prisoner's back, yes, but they are the
ones touched, their hands the ones touching:

It is important to forget your friends' names, cries at
dusk, children playing, a girl with bloody knees, a boy in
the woods, hiding:

It is dangerous to think: memory now will not help you:

We need no philosophers here, *why and why*, no
counterfactuals—your mother, your father, and one eye
gone:

How did that happen:

Years too late, we need no questions—Sam, Troy,
Everett, Riley—no mitigating circumstances: the man
doesn't want your love—your love or rage make no
difference—he wants to be a man among men, to walk
with you, to sing, to touch, *was blind but now*, to be your
companion:

His life depends on you—no mistakes, no fumbling—
no opportunity to bolt or flail, no temptation—no
pepper spray in the face, no reason to fall and fling, to
hurt, to bring you down, to die before he dies:

Your arms could choke, your weight could crush him:

So many things can go wrong—now, and later: the 7th
man stabbed again and again—every vein collapsed:
all those years pushing drugs into himself, and now the
needle stabs the hand, the leg, the neck—*we'll have to
cut to hit a vein:*

And the man laid out, strapped tight, soon to be dead
says: *no, here, let me help you:*

It is dangerous to doubt, to drive away after dark, to
think, to remember, to go home, to sit alone in the dark,
to pop the light in the kitchen:

You are not responsible:

He sang all day—your self dissolved—his voice was
everything: bone and blood: he came inside: he touched
you everywhere:

Leonard Loy Hayes, he confessed: *I wouldn't do it now,
but the way I was then, it was bound to happen:*

Addicted to meth and crack, no cash, three days, *was blind, crazy*: he'd been sniffing varnish and glue, *burning myself to scorch the pain*—he showed me the scars:

Arms and legs—burns, needles:

I should have used the knife on myself, but I slit the strap of the woman's purse, stabbed her husband in the belly—not the wound that killed, but infection blooming after:

I didn't intend, I never imagined:

I hosed him down—I saw him naked:

Scars on his back, words carved in his buttocks:

Why and when—I asked no questions:

Five months to die, over and over—the wife's hope, the man's surrender—the infection almost gone, and then again, florid: *luck or death*, Leonard said: *if he'd lived that day, I might not be here:*

43 minutes to find a viable vein, another 59 to complete the procedure—his breath, his body: sputter and spit, that trombone: his mouth, his eyelids, Leonard Loy Hayes: chest heaving high but no air: heart barely fluttering:

We had to escort his mother from the room:

Witnesses are forbidden to rise, to weep, to curse, to wail—to seize or die—to fling themselves against the glass:

The sounds she made, I'd never heard them: a creature in the woods, some small feral thing torn out of her:

We were forced to restrain, compelled to extract her:

: :

131 men: you can't scare me now: I am always afraid,
before and after:

Any Saturday the brother of a man I killed might see
me at the hardware store, might remember me opening
the door of the witness room—my shape, my shadow
on the wall—might see my hands, now, again, and
imagine:

His brother number 29:

And there in the hardware store Daniel McFerrin might
seize a screwdriver from the bin, plunge it deep in my
kidney:

Not to kill, not to finish—just to teach me how it was
for him, watching his little brother die—how it hurt:
here and here:

He pulls the screwdriver out, stabs again: *here:* how it was following me down the long corridor, through the garden, past the yellow roses climbing a white trellis: *the smell, you can't believe, the night air:*

He stabs again: *God, the roses:*

:   :

It is the 7th day and I am the 7th man—Everett, Mick,
Sam, Riley—Neville, Troy—there's no one else: I wake
into the day and know this:

Strange, the light now through lace curtains—Lidia
in the light, becoming light—you can't believe how
beautiful my wife was:

Thirty-six the day she died, Helen twelve the day she
found her:

I didn't know what to do:

Helen, our youngest: she sat down on the bathroom
floor, closed the bathroom door—and waited:

For the light to change, the day to be done, the birds to
be quiet—waited:

Here, beside her mother—where her mother lay in her
own blood—the nose, the teeth, the arm broken:

An aneurysm burst in the brain:

No one could have known, no one could expect this—flash
and blur, a dizzy flutter—*no pain*, the doctor said:

The light dissolved: *massive hemorrhage:*

I slept on the couch because the bed, the sheets—who
could sleep there:

The couch is good, the couch is narrow—*very quick,
very peaceful*—I burned her chair in the yard, her shoes,
her pillow:

Helen, Susana—my girls in the house—there, at the
window:

Hands on the glass, mouths open:

Gone before she hit the floor:

Blood in the grout in the floor between tiles—the day,
the hour, *gone*—I scrubbed and scoured, dizzy with
fumes—I could fall, I could die here—I opened the
window wide, but the birds—I didn't want to see, I
didn't want to hear them:

Years and years and years after:

And even now, today, and the light, and the curtain, and
the shadow on the floor, the way the light moves, the
way the curtain flutters:

My daughters grown and gone, their mother dead nine
years—and now, again, this morning:

I wake in the house alone—a man has a choice, a man
has his freedom: I can go to work, *die like a man*, or I
can stay here: free to drive to my brother's house, hide
in his basement—make the damp room my home, my
hole—*life without parole*: solitary confinement:

Free in my cell with myself: no hands in the dark,
no voices to touch me: no one to love, no words to
remember: *I thought you'd die:*

My mother in the dark: *I thought I'd lost you:*

Not remember: a cool rag on my face—my small self
gone and returned: six days burning with fever:

Not remember my father—black grass, the scorched
field—a field of bloated cows, legs stiff in the air, the air
smoke, the sun choked red behind it:

What could breathe:

One calf alive, ears and tail gone, eyes too swollen to see,
charred flesh peeling off her:

The sudden weight of the shotgun: my father giving me
the gun:

It's time you learned how to do this:

A free man—I can shower alone—no one to stop, no
one to watch me:

Drink coffee with cream—scramble eggs, fry bacon—
sop the grease with bread, or go to work hungry:

I can crank the radio in the truck, let sound blast
through, let sound destroy me:

A free man, it's true—but at 5:00 I'll be in the cell, at
6:06 strapped to the gurney:

Repentance now will not save: mercy here not possible:

:   :

All appeals denied: I have no right to know what drugs
will pulse into my veins, where and how the state
procured them:

*The identities of our suppliers cannot be disclosed—you
understand, for their protection:*

We cannot say who will push the drugs: a wizard behind
the wall, paid in cash, no way to find him:

The lines of your IVs snake through a tiny window:

You will not see: he cannot know you:

No pain, we can assure, but if there is you won't remember:

Stabbed again and again—Leonard Loy Hayes: 43
minutes to find a viable vein, 26 to push the drugs—
buried alive, blood on fire:

My hand on his back, his voice in my body:

I knew every cell of the heart: I felt each cell erupting:

33 minutes more to complete the procedure:

:   :

5:59—at last, already:

No fumbling now: it is very important to keep the time,
follow the steps, observe the protocol:

The warden comes first: to sense doubt or distain—
frenzy, terror, a tremor in the voice—to know if a man
will choose to walk or if he'll need to be extracted:

Mr. Arnoux, we'll proceed: are you ready:

Yes, my friends are here: they've come to take me:

No shackles or cuffs: *a man has his freedom:*

I choose to walk like a man, but the left leg's in spasm:

Very quick: this won't hurt, no:

This will kill me:

The sun choked red: black grass crackling:

What could breathe:

My father offering the gun:

It's time you learned how to do this:

These men, my friends: the breath of each man, the
heat, the heart:

We are not to blame: we fulfill our duty:

The air they move: dark blood throbbing:

We can't stop now: the door is open:

The warden close behind, watching the hip, the spine,
the sway, the stagger:

Mr. Arnoux, please sit on the gurney:

6:02—blood in the vein, green numbers pulsing:

Lie down on the pillow, please:

The gun kicks hard: the left eye twitches:

I stretch my arms wide on the arms of the gurney:

Sound destroys: the eye burns red: the green clock buzzes:

Left leg, right shoulder: Sam has the chest, Mick straps the pelvis:

The wounded calf kneels in black grass: her blind eyes see, her whole heart knows me:

Neville leans into the ribs, Riley cinches hard:

To get the job done, to be sure, to complete this:

Blood spills in the grass, the heart huge, blood pumping:

And my father takes the gun, shoots again, to be finished:

39 seconds: breath and smoke: my friends vanish:

But their weight is here: shoulder, pelvis, *as long as life endures,* the shape of each hand: leg and belly:

Only the warden now, the warden standing behind, watching the clock and me, counting seconds:

:   :

Two humans wearing masks appear: they look very
clean—one tall, one narrow: blue scrubs, the smell of
soap—human beings dressed as doctors:

They do not speak: I cannot know them:

*Please, your names, your faces, let me hear you say, let me
see you:*

They wrap rubber tubes around my arms, wait for veins
to pop, prepare to penetrate my veins, find the perfect
place to open: they swab my arms with alcohol:

So sweet the touch, their touch so tender: I have no
right to ask: *how many times have you come to this room:
how many veins like mine have you entered:*

I've walked 131 men down this hall: Willie, I confess:
we walked through the valley of the shadow of death: I
hosed you down: I saw you naked:

Doubt now will not save: hesitation here is not useful:

*Due process does not demand that every conceivable step
be taken at whatever cost to eliminate the possibility of
convicting an innocent person:*

Willie Jay McFerrin, twenty-eight years old, IQ 87: he
wanted to pray: he asked me to help him: *I fear no evil:*

Who knows if he choked that girl:

*Errors of fact discovered after a constitutionally fair trial do
not require judicial remedy:*

Sophia Stetter, five days gone: Willie found her again
or for the first time: half buried in leaves and dirt—dirt
in her mouth and eyes: *she smelled so bad, and the dirt in
her mouth: I didn't like it:*

Willie Jay dragged her into the woods: tried to stop the
smell: covered her with sticks and rags, set the rags and
sticks on fire:

Fifteen hours of interrogation: no food, no sleep, no
prayers, no lawyer:

*My brother Willie was afraid of the dark: he slept with me:
he slept with our sisters:*

Fifteen hours: the detectives told him the story over and
over: how he pummeled and choked: *you wanted to kiss,*
you wanted to love her:

And the dusk, the dark, the day done—I was afraid:

The trees, yes: I wanted to burn, I wanted to hide her:

Fifteen hours: until he believed, until he saw his small
hands on her white throat: until Willie Jay McFerrin felt
himself lift and choke and shake and snap her:

Willie: 5-foot-4, 122 pounds:

Sophia Marie: 146, three inches taller:

You tell me how my brother did this:

I didn't go home that night—my wife, my daughters—I
didn't want to see: light from the porch, the limbs of
trees, a tire swing dangling in the dark—and the smell,
my God, the roses:

Didn't want to hear: voices from another room, muffled
words, two little girls in their bedroom, laughing:

I drove to my brother's house: I hid in his basement—
scoured and scrubbed my skin—blood in the grout,
down the drain, in the shower:

Holy, holy, holy night:

:   :

I am afraid everywhere: afraid of a woman with dark
skin, bare brown thighs, soft brown belly—I follow her
in the grocery store: she feels me close—she knows: skin
on skin: *make me whole:* I want to touch her:

No, never: my eyes, my hands: for crimes committed and
imagined it is my day to die, the 7th man strapped to
the gurney:

My throat burns:

131 men: I heard your last words: your voices entered
my skull, *how sweet the sound:* I loved the sound: I go
listening for you everywhere:

Just one more thing—please: one drink of water:

The warden refuses this:

We're done here: we're finished:

He removes his glasses—a signal, a sign: permission
to the wizard behind the wall, the one who waits—
unknown, unnamed—who pushes drugs into the tubes,
who does not love, who never sees me:

What he offers now flows through tubes, snakes out this
window, ignites as it hits the vein:

*Pentobarbital will kill a horse: if there's pain, you won't
remember:*

I do remember: sky scorched red, front legs folding—no
air: chest heaving high, heart barely fluttering—the girl,
the calf, Leonard, Willie—remember as if I saw: Helen
in the bathroom, waiting for the light to change, there,
on the floor, with her mother:

:   :

My friends return: never in my life have I been so glad
to see them:

Strange to feel their hands, to think I might be dead, my
body here, my body conscious:

Beautiful to love them, to forgive, to know their hands,
to be so grateful, to hear buckles undone, *my friends*, to
feel leather straps loosen, to lie limp, dead weight, to be
dead, to surrender:

They slide their hands under—Troy, Everett, Riley—
lightly lift, gently move me: one gurney to another—
Neville, Sam, Mick:

I'm alive: the hearts I hear my own, the breath my
breath: the men I love wheel me out of here:

Silent, holy:

Now we are prepared to kill: now we are ready:

I am the 7th of 7 men: no more rehearsals:

Four nights of peace and then together my friends and I will strap down and sedate, paralyze and poison, stop the heart, end the grief, annihilate the mind of Aureo Montoya:

Please, tell me: where do we go: who do we touch, after:

Father, husband: Aureo Montoya robbed a liquor store, pulled a woman from her car, sped off with her baby— hit an old man in the street—snapped his spine, cracked his pelvis—left an old man to die:

Ditched the car: ditched the baby:

Two kids, my wife pregnant—no heat at home: a rathole with a roof—the landlord threatening to evict us:

Five hundred could have saved our lives—but as you see that didn't happen:

Aureo Montoya shot and killed a policeman's dog:

She had me by the throat: I thought she'd rip my face off:

All is calm: we will kill this man: *very quick, very peaceful:*

:   :

And then I was driving home, dusk: almost home:
nineteen miles:

I remembered a voice in the bathroom, a face in the
mirror—not my face—a face behind—I had no face:

I mean I didn't want to see my face: I was dead—it was
crazy:

No one shined a light in my eyes: no one listened for a
heartbeat:

I was dead or not dead:

No needles in my veins—no need to remove them: the
medical team did not return: even now, they keep their
secrets:

Only my friends appeared, weirdly quiet, unwilling
to look me in the eyes as they slid their hands, as they
cradled my body:

The gurney rolled—lights too loud, lights blazing—my head a hive, fingers buzzing:

Then here we were, safe in the hallway:

Mick gripped my hand and pulled: I remember the body sitting tall, the body straight on the gurney: I felt my feet hit the floor—here I was—I was standing:

Alive as Lazarus, someone said, voice bouncing wall to wall, rib to rib inside me:

Alive to die again, not knowing when or why the next time:

Then the face, a blur, Mick behind me in the bathroom: *grab a beer*, he must have said: and something like my voice said, *not tonight, catch you later*:

I remember splashing water on my face, feeling my face with my hands, water flowing between fingers:

In the car, the smell: piss and blood, an open wound, the mouth infected—shit smeared, blood spilled—the skull slammed into a wall, the weeping wall, the body open:

Your voices throbbed in my chest:

2329 human beings, all these men, human waste kept in
cages: the walls and floor concrete, concrete permeable:
you can't scrub, can't scour, can't bleach the skin—the
smell inside and out—skin of the naked self, the self
permeable:

It's true: I did these things—robbed, choked, hit, killed—
yes, I shot the dog: but I never hurt the baby:

The men in the car, with me, the smell everywhere:

Aureo Montoya: six years in prison and free to work on
the prison farm:

A slave in the sun: and there I was, and there he was, and
the stick I'd found was sharp, and the sun in my eyes, and
the stick in my hand, and he was close and hot, hotter than
the day, and the light, and I must have stabbed him in the
throat: the stick was in the throat, in the vein, and I pulled
it out, and the blood, and then I was in the dirt, pinned
down on my face, two guards grinding me to the ground,
and he kept spurting blood, dying in the dirt, dying right
beside me:

What you say must be true:

As long as I'm alive nobody is safe here:

I rolled the windows down, let the dusk come in, let the cold take me:

What he did to me I won't confess: when I'm dead three days, I'll come back and tell you:

:   :

So slow I was, swerving to the side of the road—letting
wind blow, letting gravel jolt me—pulling back into my
lane, every car surging past, every human being passing:

Orange flare of a cigarette, a man alone, smoke and dust:
my father alive, but moving fast: a woman with a little
dog in her lap, the dog's dark head out the window:

A husband and wife leaning apart—something said or
unsaid—not yet and maybe never:

Please: children crushed in the backseat, four or five—
everyone undone—climbing over and back, one side to
another:

Forgive him now: you never know what will happen:

I saw houses full of light, bodies moving behind
curtains—breath and smoke: broken teeth, brains on
fire—jack o' lanterns grinning from the steps:

Faces torn, skulls empty: a church with a neon cross:

Light of the Redeemer: two bars flashing their names:
Last Chance, Merle's Refuge:

Blisters of light between trees: shacks along a winding
path: a house alone, an open field:

Something had happened here, but no one knew—they
couldn't see it—or it was happening now, coming into
being this very moment—a darker place where darkness
gathered: a shadow crossing the earth—clouds hiding
the moon—nothing more: dust and smoke, clouds and
field, forests of oak and pine: the world at dusk, driving
through it:

But the shape had life and form, vast breath—
something close and dark—a herd of cattle moving as
one, as if in flight, as if fire—*no:*

Too fast, too quiet—the shadow becoming deer, a wave
of living beings, not yet bedded down, awake and alive,
suddenly startled: watched from the woods by bobcat or
cougar:

And then they too were behind, and it was impossible
to know, now or ever, and the rumble strip bounced me
back into my lane:

Almost home: sixteen miles:

:   :

No light spilling from the porch, no swing, no voices—
no reason to be afraid, no shadows behind curtains:

The couch is good, the couch is narrow: you can stand
in the shower all night: let water scald, let water numb
you:

And then I saw them: a family in another car, not
passing—traveling along beside, moving with me:

A man and a girl in the front seat, a baby in back,
strapped in a car seat: a man and his child bride, or a
man and his daughter—the baby her son, the baby her
brother—I wanted to know:

The answer to this seemed very important:

Voices in the car blurred—I swear I could hear: too
many voices at once, the man arguing with himself—
repeating, rewinding—too many words, words
overlapping—and then something else:

The girl playing piano in her mind, hearing each note—
call and response—each note pulsing through us:

Reverberation in the throat and heart—alto, soprano—
Lidia and her sister Florence: they could both sing
either line—my wife, her echo:

And I knew before I knew—the stuttering heart, breath
catching: the stagger when you start to fall—blood in
the brain—the sudden weight of the self, the snap of
bone, bone cracking:

And even now, the girl in the car playing piano that
way—two melodies at once, breaking into separate
tempos:

A bird singing two songs:

How could she:

And still the car did not pass, but the music faded—
wind, pines, distant fire—the man's argument swelled,
the baby whimpered:

The girl unbuckled her belt, turned, leaned over the
seat—touched the baby's face—her hands, her fingers—
my face: *shush, almost home:*

Almost home, fourteen miles:

Voices stabbed the man's skull—jolts of light, vessels
bursting—adrenaline shooting down the spine:

Gone, the car surged: the ones I love far beyond me—
over a hill, around a curve: *shush*, the soft voice, the
strange music, the baby's cry, the man's curses—gone:
but the heart hurt—no air, lungs heaving:

I gripped the wheel hard, to stay on the road, to stay
steady:

Then the road straight, but so many lights the lights
blurred and I didn't know the girl's light from any other:

A rise and dip in the road—everyone gone—only the
dark, the shapes of trees, deeper darkness—*no one,
nothing*—my lights too dim:

I can't find you:

Then too much all at once, flares of white light—
everything wrong—cars jumping lanes—light blasting:

Nowhere to go but over and down—rolling now, down
the gully:

:   :

Blood rushed to my head: it took some time to think, to reason—my head hurt, my head too heavy:

Gasoline leaking in the grass, sparks flickering from the engine:

My body dangling upside down—I would die strapped in, burn if I stayed here:

A man alone, hanging from a seatbelt:

I tucked my head to my chest, loosened the strap an inch at a time, eased myself down to the roof, kept my head tucked, released the belt and rolled, crawled out the window:

How far could the road be:

But it was far, the sound of cars a distant river, all their
lights obscured, no way to know, no lights to follow—
no light of stars—only the moon drifting between
clouds, illuminating clouds, a ring of gold and orange—
showing half its face, and disappearing:

Sirens howled, wailed into the night from two
directions: rose up through earth, through bone, then
faded:

The moon bright and gone, stars unseen, dogs barking:

High and fast and far away—another low and close—a
third one growling:

One wild in the woods: the mockingbird mocking:

You are the ones: I thought the dogs would smell me
here, find me in the grass—lie down or lead me to
the road—howl till humans came, till human voices
touched me:

Only the bird continued: becoming a pack of dogs, the
opossum hissing—crickets and frogs—the crow, the
sparrow—scolding then breaking into song—warbling
in its own voice, whimpering like a child:

I wasn't hurt—I could crawl—I could stand—left leg
weak but I could walk—I could climb—find a stick to
support—get back to the road and wait—or rest, or
sleep, or die here:

I heard the first sputtering notes of a trombone: the
mockingbird tempting me toward the woods, into the
dark, away from the road, and I thought, *no, not here: I
saw you die: I killed you:*

But Leonard, I loved that sound: I'd been listening for
you everywhere:

The shapes of trees seemed kind—leaves trembling
in the dark, needles whistling—they loved me, they
knew—in every hidden ring a year we'd shared: our
lives, our secrets:

I stumbled toward the grove, deeper and deeper into
it—I was not afraid of the dark—I grabbed limbs as I
walked, felt vines of wisteria:

Tupelo and pine, hickory, maple: they remembered
me hiding here, that thin, fatherless boy—that quick,
quiet child—I loved this damp earth, trees so close they
blocked the sun:

I might meet an alligator here, a gray fox climbing a
tree—a bat, a skunk, a flying squirrel—deep in the
Piney Woods: black snakes and white deer—God, now,
imagining the world:

I buried myself in leaves and needles, dead for an hour
or a day, a boy so lost in the woods not even light could
find me:

And now, again, the moon behind clouds, the clouds
beyond trees, the voices of owls:

How sweet the sound:

I must have closed my eyes—but I didn't sleep, I swear:
I didn't move, I promise:

:   :

Safe and still, so little difference between breathing and
not breathing:

But I did breathe, choked and gasped, a cloud of smoke
clotting the lung, dirt in the mouth and eyes—the world
becoming smoke and fire:

The air had a voice: throat torn, bowels burning:

I smelled the bodies of trees—not just ash but charred
wood—pieces of trees raining down:

I heard the cries of cows all night:

The earth, the sky, the air dissolved:

Nothing breathed: I stood at the window—hands on
the glass, mouth open—refused to go outside: *no, never:*
denied what I saw:

Backhoes digging a trench, bloated cows dragged and
hoisted—a holocaust of cows—dropped in the trench,
bodies bursting:

Everything lost: the cows, the field—black grass,
charred fences: the house spared by fire but sold:

For nothing, my father said: we moved 596 miles east,
lived in a little town, rented a house in town where my
father stared at birds:

As if he wanted to kill, as if they had done this:

Everything strange—the tiny yard, flowering
dogwood—no one could explain:

My father working as a janitor at the school where I
went to school: he hated leaving the house at dusk,
scrubbing all night, scouring toilets, bleaching urinals,
erasing equations he could never comprehend, scraping
graffiti from stalls, reading our smut, our rage, our
ridiculous obscenities—entering our minds night
after night, smelling our bodies in the dark—feeling
our small hands on the walls, and then our hands as
we shoved him in our spit, tripped him to his knees,
pushed him face down in our filth, tied him with string,
wrapped it round and round till he couldn't move, till
we could write the words, our words, in his mind, on his
body:

It must have felt like that, night after night, alone with
our grit and sweat, laughter in the walls, whispers
festering:

I never asked: he never spoke of it:

Even when I saw my father starved, my father wasted—
when we knew: the esophagus scorched, the cancer
florid:

And then one day I was sitting in my classroom, a weird
day, a sudden snow storm, and it was cold that day
where I was by the window, and there was snow hitting
the glass, snow melting, snow blowing hard outside,
snow whirling:

So amazed, I was, alive but trapped here: the teacher
reading words: expecting us to spell them:

Abandon, defile, refuge, resuscitate:

Who knows what she said: *abound, ablaze, defy,
annihilate:*

I wrote nothing on the page: *refuse, resist, deny, extirpate:*

It was wrong to sit, to be, to wait here: the snow so
close, so strange, so miraculous—it never snowed like
this—in the twelve long years of my life, never: and here
I sat, strapped, *bound*, *ablaze*, shackled:

And I saw him, a shivering man in a ragged coat,
hunched against the snow—a thin man with bare
hands, hands too big for his shrunken body:

Refute, redeem: why should he be free: *recoil:*

He must have felt my fire—the old man raised his head
and turned, stared back at me, took my fury:

I knew that man:

He looked away, pretended not to see, ashamed of
himself or me: he must have fallen asleep in the boiler
room, must have been curled there all morning, a heap
of sticks and rags, my father—must have heard children
in the hallway—shouts, stomping boots—must have
waited for us to go, to file into our classrooms—tried
to stand but been too tired—slept again and just
awakened:

Deny, refuse:

There was no one to hate but myself, no way to go home and confess, no words to explain, after:

No way to look at the face across the table, to hear my father chew and try to swallow, to see him choke and gag and spit in the sink—this horrible old man, forty-four years old:

The soon to be dead shall receive no pleasure:

Now here I was, older than my father: mouth full of dirt, too weak to walk, half buried: the mockingbird pretending to be an owl, the smell of smoke years gone, my hands numb, the grass slippery:

My brother and I dug a hole for our father: I lay down in that hole, stared at stars, tried to imagine:

Early June, already scorching:

I slept in the earth:

I woke hot in the dirt, and that day we buried our father:

:   :

We buried my wife:

:   :

We buried our mother:

:   :

Between tall trees, I saw a flicker of light—imagined a
house, a bed, a blanket—a human being with human
hands: someone alive, someone waiting:

Clouds opened: the moon showed half its face, and I
watched my own hands touch my own body:

The light seemed far but not too far:

The mockingbird's song kept my heart throbbing:

I crawled between trees, in the dark, in the shadows—
smelled piss and blood—my skin, myself—the body
open:

Felt again or for the first time a clot breaking free,
the pressure in the chest, my mother kneeling in the
garden—lying down to rest, *here,* suddenly so tired:

My father thirty-two years gone:

And now my mother in the dirt, in the day, with her flowers:

A wave of yellow birds warbling in flight:

I tried to stand: the birds insisted:

My mother alive: minutes or hours:

Three deer watching from the trees:

The songs of birds:

The cool earth, the smell of roses:

And now, today: the deer watching me, leading me out of the trees:

And then: the deer returning at dusk to eat my mother's roses:

:   :

Listen: I crawled out of the forest on my hands and
knees:

With the new day and its impossible light falling all
around us, I staggered across this broken field:

Now I stand swaying at the side of the road—dirt in
my eyes and throat—a man half dead, a man who's been
buried—dirt in the shell of the skull, dirt heaped high
in the open belly:

Listen: with the bodies of birds trembling into song:

I confess:

I failed to love:

I dragged: I strapped: I killed: I poisoned:

I stopped your hearts:

Over and over:

With the deer quiet in the field, a man too weak to
stand—as cars rush by, as wind blows him—is falling to
his knees in the gravel at the side of the road, waiting for
you—mother, brother, child of a man I killed—waiting,
I confess, for you to swerve and stop, sing my name,
touch my face, stab to kill, pierce and amaze me:

ACKNOWLEDGMENTS

I am grateful to the Lannan Foundation for providing sanctuary in Marfa, Texas. I am also grateful to the National Endowment for the Arts; Corby Skinner and the Writer's Voice Project in Billings, Montana; the Utah Arts Council; Bob Goldberg and the Tanner Humanities Center; and the University of Utah. The faith of these individuals and the support of these institutions have made my work possible. Thank you.

For their abiding love and unwavering belief, their extraordinary contributions to research, and their joyful, generous reading, I thank my family. Dear Gary, Glenna, Laurie, Wendy, Tom, Melinda, Nathan, Kelsey, Amanda, Chris, Mike, Sami, Brad, Alyssa, Hayley—Dear Mom, dear Father even now and always—Dear Cleora, Randy, Alicia, Valerie, Kimmer, Kristi—Dear Jan and John: your love, your beautiful lives are the radiance within all stories.

I thank Jill Patterson, Valerie Sayers, Tami Haaland, Randy Schwickert, and Katy Ryan for their companionship, and for their miraculous work in the world.

To my students who teach and transform me, Thank you.

By the faith and companionship, love, insight and inspiration of my dear friends and early readers—Lance and Andi Olsen, Kate Coles, Fiona McCrae, Irene Skolnick, Tessa Fontaine, and Mary Pinard—I am endlessly and forever blessed.

I thank Ander Monson and the staff at New Michigan Press for their kindness and expertise, their exquisite work on this book and their generous work in the world.

MELANIE RAE THON'S most recent books are *Silence & Song*, the novel *The Voice of the River*, and *In This Light: New and Selected Stories*. She is also the author of the novels *Sweet Hearts, Meteors in August*, and *Iona Moon*, and the story collections *First, Body* and *Girls in the Grass*. She is a recipient of a Whiting Writer's Award, two fellowships from the National Endowment for the Arts, the Mountains & Plains Independent Booksellers Association Reading the West Book Award, the Gina Berriault Award, the Utah Book Award, and a Writer's Residency from the Lannan Foundation. In 2009, she was Virgil C. Aldrich Fellow at the Tanner Humanities Center. Originally from Montana, Melanie now lives in Salt Lake City, where she teaches in the Creative Writing and Environmental Humanities programs at the University of Utah.

: :

COLOPHON

Text is set in a digital version of Jenson, designed by Robert Slimbach in 1996, and based on the work of punchcutter, printer, and publisher Nicolas Jenson. The titles are in Futura.

:   :

NEW MICHIGAN PRESS, based in Tucson, Arizona,
prints poetry and prose chapbooks, especially
work that transcends traditional genre. Together
with DIAGRAM, NMP sponsors a yearly chapbook
competition.

DIAGRAM, a journal of text, art, and schematic,
is published bimonthly at THEDIAGRAM.COM.
Periodic print anthologies are available from the New
Michigan Press at NEWMICHIGANPRESS.COM.

CPSIA information can be obtained at www.ICGtesting.com
Printed in the USA
LVOW07s1128290116

472874LV00003B/59/P